THE TRANSFORMERS™

MORE THAN MEETS THE EYE!

THE AUTOBOTS' SECRET WEAPON

Written by Nancy Krulik
Illustrated by Charles Nicholas
and Roberta Edelman

AUTOBOT

DECEPTICON

MARVEL BOOKS

ISBN 0-87135-061-0

It was a bright, sunny day. Sunstreaker, the vainest of all the Autobots, was lying by the river, staring at his own reflection in the water. Sunstreaker loved to watch himself change from robot to car and back again.

"I am the best looking Autobot around," Sunstreaker told himself. "Especially when my metal is freshly shined!"

The he pulled out some wax and a rag and began shining his chrome.

Sunstreaker was so busy shining himself that he didn't notice that someone had sneaked up right behind him.

"Hey, you, get out of my light," said Sunstreaker.

As he turned around, Sunstreaker gasped. Behind him was the biggest Decepticon he had ever seen!

The giant Decepticon reached for Sunstreaker. Quickly Sunstreaker transformed into his sports car form and tried to drive away. But the giant Decepticon was too fast for Sunstreaker. He had reached out his huge leg and stepped on Sunstreaker's fenders.

"That's it!" cried Sunstreaker. "Mess up my chrome and it's war!"

Sunstreaker quickly transformed back to his robot form. Even though his metal was dented, he still had all of his Autobot powers. He shot laser after laser at the giant Decepticon. But the Decepticon was quick. He avoided all of Sunstreaker's missile attacks.

Sunstreaker was powerless against the Decepticon. Hard as he fought, the Decepticon fought harder. For every missile Sunstreaker shot, the Decepticon shot six!

Finally, Sunstreaker was too weary from the battle to move. That's when the giant Decepticon scooped Sunstreaker up and brought him to the hideout of the evil Decepticons!

The gigantic Decepticon threw Sunstreaker into a prison cell and locked the door. Sunstreaker tried using his Autobot strength to shake the bars loose, but they wouldn't budge. Then he shot his laser rockets at the bars, but they wouldn't melt. Sunstreaker was stuck! Sadly he sat down in a corner of the cell.

Suddenly Sunstreaker saw something he had never seen before. The giant Decepticon was breaking apart. First the arms came off. Then the legs broke away from the body. Finally the head and shoulders dropped to the ground. There were six pieces in all. Each piece became a separate Decepticon!

One of the Decepticons walked over to the cell and looked at Sunstreaker.

"We are the Constructicons," he said. "Separately we have the same amount of power as any of our fellow Decepticons. But when we join forces, we become Devastator, one of the most powerful robots of all! The Autobots are helpless against Devastator!"

Just then Megatron, leader of the Decepticons, walked into the prison. He went over to the cell and sneered at Sunstreaker. Sunstreaker sneered back at Megatron.

"Very good, Constructicons," said Megatron. "You have captured an Autobot. Now I know my plan will work. In just a few hours, the Autobots will surrender! We will rule the Earth!"

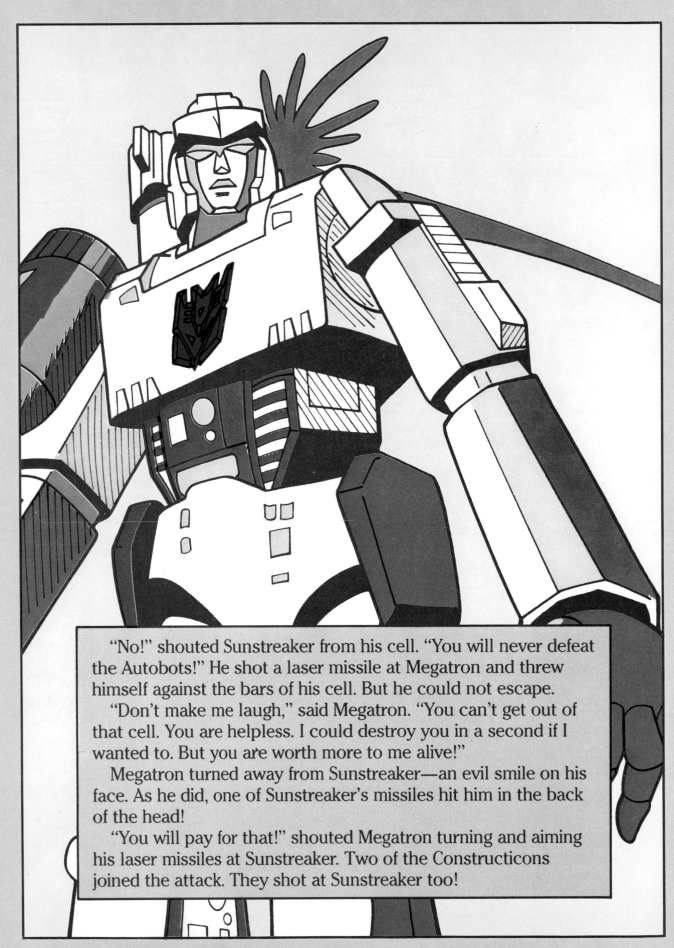

"No!" shouted Sunstreaker from his cell. "You will never defeat the Autobots!" He shot a laser missile at Megatron and threw himself against the bars of his cell. But he could not escape.

"Don't make me laugh," said Megatron. "You can't get out of that cell. You are helpless. I could destroy you in a second if I wanted to. But you are worth more to me alive!"

Megatron turned away from Sunstreaker—an evil smile on his face. As he did, one of Sunstreaker's missiles hit him in the back of the head!

"You will pay for that!" shouted Megatron turning and aiming his laser missiles at Sunstreaker. Two of the Constructicons joined the attack. They shot at Sunstreaker too!

Sunstreaker tried to fight back, but they were too much for him. Finally he crawled into a corner of his cell and tried to tend his wounds.

Megatron laughed at Sunstreaker and called for Soundwave, the Decepticon communicator.

"Soundwave, prepare to transmit a message," he said. "Tell the Autobots that we have captured Sunstreaker. Then tell the Decepticons that tomorrow we will have a big gathering. We will celebrate the defeat of the Autobots!"

Meanwhile, back at the Autobot camp, the Autobots were waiting for Sunstreaker. They were beginning to worry about him. "I hope Sunstreaker isn't in any danger," said Optimus Prime, leader of the Autobots. "It isn't like him to be away for so long!"

"Quiet, everyone," shouted Blaster, the Autobot communicator. "I am receiving a message from the Decepticons."

The Autobots grew silent and listened to the message.
"Optimus Prime, this is Megatron. We have captured
Sunstreaker. It is useless for you to try and rescue him. All
Autobots are defenseless against the mighty Devastator!
"Unless you surrender and agree to leave Earth, Sunstreaker
will be destroyed! Then we will rebuild him as a Decepticon! You
have until sunrise to give up!"

"Surrender! Never!" shouted Sideswipe. "Sunstreaker is my twin Autobot. I will go and rescue him myself!"

"But you cannot defeat Devastator alone," said Grimlock. "Sludge and Slag will go too. Your powers, along with our Dinobot strength, will give us all the force we need to defeat Devastator!"

Optimus Prime looked worried. He did not want to lose any more Autobots to Devastator.

"Before you go," he said, "I must tell you about Devastator. He is not an ordinary Decepticon. He is really six Constructicons put together. It will take all our strength and cleverness to defeat Devastator!"

"Don't worry," said Slag. "It's true we've never fought anything like Devastator before. But Devastator has never battled the Dinobots either!"

With that, Slag, Sludge and Sideswipe headed for the Decepticon hideout.

The Decepticons had set traps all along the long road to the hideout. Sideswipe drove right into a land mine! There was a giant explosion. Sideswipe was thrown into the air! He flipped over. For a second, it looked as if Sideswipe would land on his roof and burst into flames.

But just in time, Sideswipe transformed to his robot form. He used his powerful arms to break his fall. Sideswipe was safe!

Quickly he transformed back to car mode and he and the Dinobots continued to the Decepticon camp.

As Slag, Sludge and Sideswipe arrived at the Decepticon hideout, they were stopped by two Decepticon guards.

"You can't come in here," said one of the guards.

"Wanna bet?" replied Slag. Then the three Autobots transformed into robots. They began to attack the Decepticon guards with their laser missiles!

The guards shot back! One guard shot a missile straight at Sideswipe. But Sideswipe was too fast. He transformed to his car form and drove right into the knees of the Decepticon guard. The guard collapsed.

The other Decepticon guard turned to see what had happened. Slag and Sludge zapped him with their awesome Dinobot weapons.

The guards were too weak to fight anymore.

Slag, Sludge, and Sideswipe had won their first battle!

But there were many more battles to go. They still had to face Devastator!

They ran swiftly into the Decepticon camp. All at once they stopped dead in their tracks. In front of them was the most terrible sight they had ever seen—DEVASTATOR. He towered over them and sneered as if he was daring them to attack first!

Slag took the first shot. He raised his powerful arm and fired a powerful Dinobot missile. It was a hit! The Decepticon looked to be hurt. Slag relaxed a little. Maybe he had actually beaten this monster!

But Slag was wrong. His shot had just made Devastator angry. He reached out his leg and kicked Slag to the ground.

Sludge tried to come to Slag's rescue. He shot a missile at the head of the giant Decepticon. But Devastator fired back. Four missiles zoomed straight at Sludge!

Slag jumped to his feet and tried to use his Dinobot strength to wrestle Devastator to the ground. But the Decepticon kept firing at Slag. The Dinobot was powerless.

Then Sideswipe tried to attack Devastator the way he had defeated the Decepticon guard. He transformed to car mode and drove straight for Devastator's leg. But Devastator just stuck out his giant arm and stopped Sideswipe. Then he scooped up all three Autobots and brought them to Sunstreaker's cell.

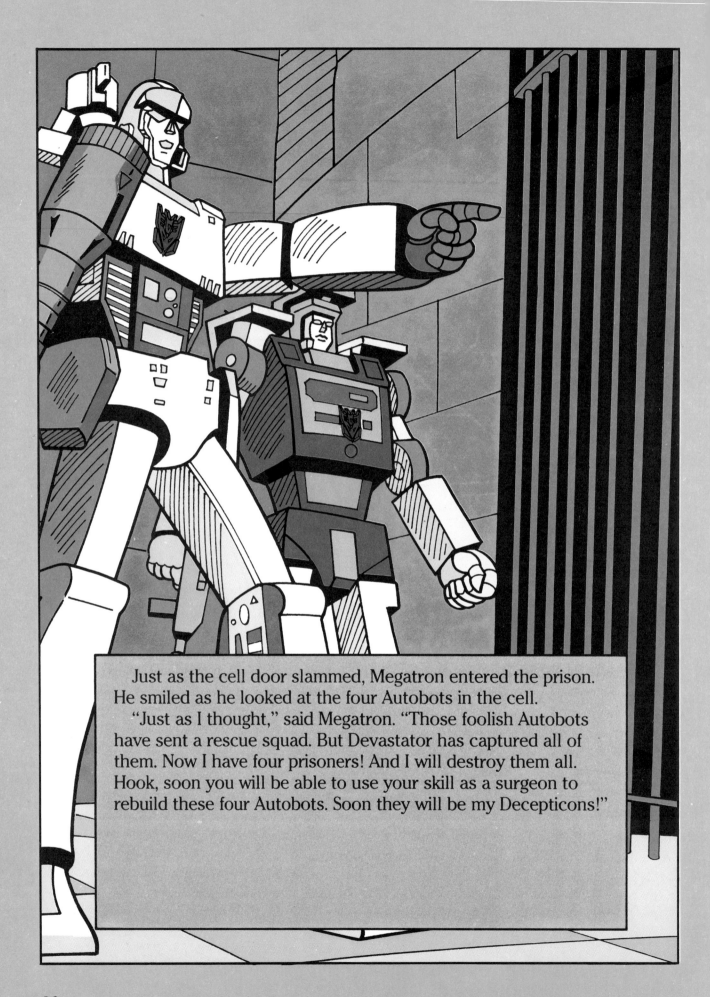

Just as the cell door slammed, Megatron entered the prison. He smiled as he looked at the four Autobots in the cell.

"Just as I thought," said Megatron. "Those foolish Autobots have sent a rescue squad. But Devastator has captured all of them. Now I have four prisoners! And I will destroy them all. Hook, soon you will be able to use your skill as a surgeon to rebuild these four Autobots. Soon they will be my Decepticons!"

"Can I crush these Autobots into little pieces?" asked Bonecrusher, one of the Constructicons.

"No way," shouted Hook, another Constructicon. "I want to use my laser pistol to destroy them. After all, I am the one who will be rebuilding these Autobots as Decepticons! I want to do the destroying!"

Then Bonecrusher reached out and tried to tackle Hook. Hook slammed Bonecrusher with his arm. Soon the two Constructicons were wrestling and fighting each other!

"Stop it," yelled Megatron. "I promise you can both destroy an Autobot. But you must wait until tomorrow. At sunrise, we will defeat the Autobots once and for all!"

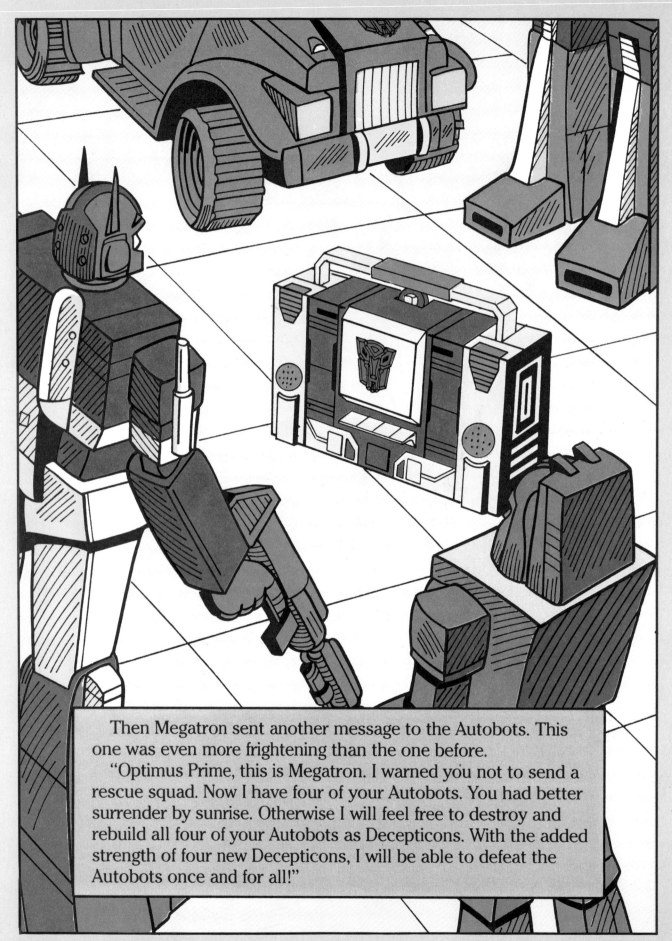

Then Megatron sent another message to the Autobots. This one was even more frightening than the one before.

"Optimus Prime, this is Megatron. I warned you not to send a rescue squad. Now I have four of your Autobots. You had better surrender by sunrise. Otherwise I will feel free to destroy and rebuild all four of your Autobots as Decepticons. With the added strength of four new Decepticons, I will be able to defeat the Autobots once and for all!"

For the first time, the Autobots were scared. It looked as though Megatron had beaten them this time. Devastator could not be stopped. Finally, Swoop, the fearsome flying Dinobot, stood up and spoke to the Dinobots.

"My fellow Autobots," he said, "I wish I could say otherwise, but we have no choice. We must surrender. We cannot join forces the way Devastator can. We must surrender to save our fellow Autobots."

"Not so fast, Swoop," said Optimus Prime. "You have given me an idea. But we will have to work very quickly. It is only a few hours until sunrise. Now gather around while I tell you all of my plan!"

The Autobots worked quickly to get Optimus Prime's secret plan ready. They worked all night long. Everything had to be absolutely perfect for the plan to work. The plan *had* to work. If it didn't it would mean the end of the Autobots forever!

Finally the Autobots were finished. A few hours before sunrise they put the plan into action.

First they sent a giant statue over to the Decepticon hideout. The statue looked like Devastator. Attached to the statue was a letter. The letter said:

"Megatron, you win. We cannot fight Devastator. We are giving you this statue as a peace offering. We surrender!"

The Decepticon guards wheeled the statue to the center of the hideout. Then they brought Megatron to see it.

Megatron looked at the statue and read the letter. Then he started to laugh.

"We have done it!" he said. "We have beaten the Autobots. The Earth is ours!"

Then Megatron ordered the Decepticons to bring the four Autobot prisoners to see the statue.

Sunstreaker, Slag, Sludge and Sideswipe could not believe the statue or the letter! They knew the Autobots would never surrender!

All heads turned as Devastator came up to the statue. Then the Decepticons cheered. Here was the greatest Decepticon of all— Devastator. He was the one that had made all of this possible. The statue was really for him.

As Devastator touched the statue's arm, there was a gasp of surprise from the Decepticons!

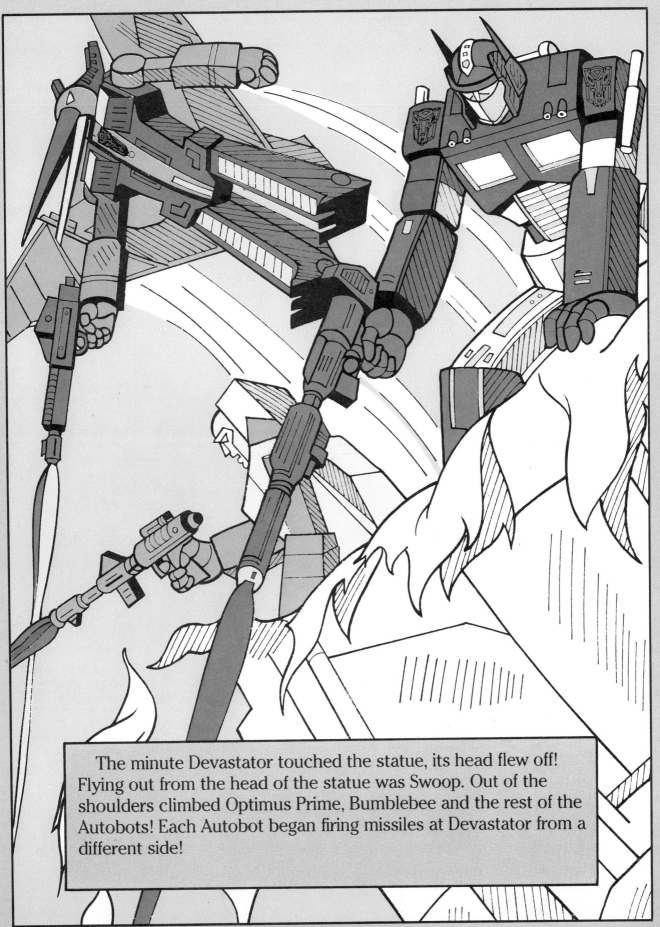

The minute Devastator touched the statue, its head flew off! Flying out from the head of the statue was Swoop. Out of the shoulders climbed Optimus Prime, Bumblebee and the rest of the Autobots! Each Autobot began firing missiles at Devastator from a different side!

Devastator was confused! Each part of his body was trying to fight in a different direction. After all, Devastator was really six different robots. Now each Constructicon was trying to fight a different Autobot.

Finally Devastator's legs broke away from his body. Then his head dropped and then his arms. Standing in the middle of the Decepticon camp were six different Decepticons instead of one giant robot. Now the battle was even!

Swoop started firing laser missiles at the Decepticons. The Decepticons were caught off guard. They were not ready for a fight. One by one they tried to aim their lasers and shoot at Swoop. But Swoop was too much for them. He dodged all of their badly aimed missiles. And he aimed his missiles perfectly.

"Take that!" he shouted. "You will never be able to destroy a Dinobot!"

"All fighter planes in the air," shouted Optimus Prime. Up went all the Autobot jets.

"Get them," yelled Megatron. Up went all the Decepticon jets.

The jets started firing at one another. There were missiles all over the sky. Orange fire lit up the sky. There were so many missiles shooting and robots falling that it was impossible to see who was winning the air fight!

On the ground, Rumble was helping the Decepticon cause. Rumble's special talent was making Earthquakes. He decided to cause the Earth to shake and swallow up all the Autobots on the ground. He jumped and he pounded and he screamed and he yelled. Then the ground cracked open. Thousands of robots were falling into the cracks! It looked like Rumble's plan had worked.

Suddenly Megatron looked over at the Earthquake.

"Stop it, you fool," he screamed. "Those are not Autobots falling into the crack. Those are Decepticons. You are wounding robots on *our* side!"

Megatron decided to end the battle once and for all. He aimed his Laser cannon right at Optimus Prime.

"This is it, Optimus Prime," he shouted. "My laser cannons will melt you down!"

Megatron shot his lasers right at Optimus Prime. Just in time, Optimus Prime grabbed a piece of shiny metal from the ground. He held the metal in front of his body. The metal deflected the laser.

Megatron screamed in pain and fell to the ground. Megatron hit himself with the laser—instead of Optimus Prime!

"Let's go, Autobots, ordered Optimus Prime. "We will gather up the bodies of our wounded and bring them back to the Ark for repair. Not even Devastator can defeat us when we work together!"

— The End —